Defending Skullpass
GUNSLINGERS VS. ZOMBIES

JUPITER DRESDEN
♡ EVELYN BELLE ♡

Evelyn Belle

ILLUSTRATED BY
EVE GRAPHIC DESIGN LLC.

Copyright © 2023 Jupiter Dresden & Evelyn Belle
Published by Jupiter Dresden & Evelyn Belle
All rights reserved.
All rights reserved. No part of this publication may be reproduced/transmitted/distributed in any form. No part of this publication shall be shared by any means including photocopying, recording, or any electronic/mechanical method, or the Internet, without prior written consent of the author. Cases of brief quotations embodied in critical reviews and certain other non-commercial uses permitted by copyright law are the exception. The unauthorized reproduction/transmitting of this work is illegal
Published in the United States of America
Edited By: Michelle's Edits
Cover By: Eve Graphic Design LLC.
Formatted By: Purrfectly Haunting Formatting

Lindsey
To one of the strongest women we know.
We love you

Contents

Prologue	1
Chapter 1	5
Chapter 2	12
Chapter 3	18
Chapter 4	23
Chapter 5	30
Chapter 6	38
Chapter 7	44
Chapter 8	49
Chapter 9	54
Chapter 10	62
Chapter 11	67
Epilogue	76
About Jupiter Dresden	79
Acknowledgments	81
Also by Jupiter Dresden	83
About Evelyn Belle	85
Also By Evelyn Belle	87

Prologue

FIVE YEARS EARLIER

The weight of the bank bags under my arms are getting heavy. I've never held this much loot at one time, unless you count the time I robbed Robert McMasters. His body outweighed this by a good fifty pounds. Flynn, Holt, and Virgil are right in front of me. Bullets are zooming all around us as we leave the bank.

"Wren! We are in a tough spot," Virgil calls back. "They have us surrounded!"

"It's us or them!" I yell back, as I let off a couple of rounds out of my revolver over their heads.

Finally after several moments, my eye catches an open section; without another thought, I make a break for it. I don't look back to see if the guys are following me or not. Tex sits at the edge of town waiting for my arrival. He whinnies at the sight of me. My breathing is labored as I stow the first money bag and work on the second one.

A bullet whizzes by my head just missing Tex. As I mount Tex, I'm not so lucky, a bullet hits me in my left shoulder. There's no time to tend to it. Right now I need to hightail it out of here. Tex and I take off like lightning, no regard for the others. My gang will catch up once on the outskirts of town.

After waiting longer than I should've at the edge of town, we take off. The men are on their own now. The loot in my bags will be my cut. Now it's time to find a town where I can lay low.

My shoulder throbs with every stride, but we can't stop. Tex can feel my pain and tries to slow down but I slap the reins letting him know to keep going.

Safety is close at hand but I don't want to get too comfortable yet. Because when I do that is when someone will pop up, then that will be my end. Tex would be lost in this shithole without me, as I would be without him.

I need to find a good town that's out of the way to lay low for a while, to get the heat off, somewhere no one knows me. Maybe a place I could reinvent myself for the time being, so no one would know I'm a bank robber. One of the most wanted women in the west.

I must have blacked out from the pain, waking up thankful to still be on Tex and he hasn't stopped. The sky is pitch black above. The moon's crescent shape giving just a little light to guide us. I pull the reins back, slowing Tex since he's got to be exhausted.

"Just a bit further. We'll get you some feed and a nice place to rest, my friend," I tell him while patting him on the shoulder. "Next town we come to we'll stay for the night."

After about another hour of riding, I can see the twinkles of lit lamps. The closer we ride the more the silhouette of a town comes into view. Not much commotion going on at this time, not sure how late it is. I'm sure once I stroll in town all bloody, I'll find out.

It feels like I've stopped bleeding, I'm hoping the bullet went straight through. If it has to be dug out, that's not going to be fun. This is something I've never enjoyed, but it comes with my line of work. Most of the men I've encountered couldn't shoot worth two shits, so most of my wounds have just been grazes.

Tex comes to a dead stop as a figure shoots out in front of us. My right hand goes straight for my gun. The man steps into the dim light, as I point my gun at his head.

"Whoa, miss, I don't want any trouble," he says, his hands up in the air.

I grit my teeth. "Then what is it you want?"

"Sorry, ma'am. I'm just the welcome party into town when it's dark. Didn't mean any harm," he replies, bringing down his arms. "You look to be in some pain. Blood and all on that arm."

"I just need a stable and a place to lay my head for the night," I tell him, slowly putting my gun up before I dismount Tex carefully. "If you can't help, please move. He's thirsty and needs rest."

"Oh no, ma'am, I know just the place. My pappy has a place you can board your horse while in town. And Miss Adeline always has an extra room. If you don't mind staying at a saloon."

"If it has a bed and somewhere to wash, I don't care," I tell him, grabbing Tex by the reins to lead him the rest of the way into town.

"She can fix you up with clean linens as well, until what you have on can be washed."

He's got so much excitement in his voice. Before any more words can be exchanged, he takes the reins from me. I want to protest but my body is beyond the point of exhaustion and this bullet wound still needs tending to.

"I'll make sure he's watered and fed, ma'am." He nods toward a building that's still lit up. "The saloon is just right there. Go in and ask for Adeline, she'll get everything set up for you."

"Where are you taking him?" I stop him with the question.

"Sorry, we'll just be down the street and take a left. There are stables there. Plenty of hay for him to eat and water for him to drink." The man points down the street in front of us.

"One more question before you go." I look him in the eyes "Why should I trust you with my horse?"

"Well, ma'am, my pappy is the sheriff, so if you can't trust the law's family then who?"

"Let me grab my bags off of Tex then you're welcome to take him. And the name's Wren, Wren Graves."

Probably not my brightest hour giving him my real name. He just seems so innocent, someone I can trust. Before I can reach for them with my good arm, he's got them off and is handing them over.

"Are you sure you can manage these, Wren? They seem heavy for one arm." Concern is in his baby-blue eyes.

"Yes, kid, this isn't my first rodeo. Won't be my last I'm sure," I explain while grabbing some coins out of my front pocket. "Here's some money to start off with. Let me know how much more I own you in the morning."

"Thank you, Wren. Sorry about my manners, I'm Levi and welcome to Skullpass."

Chapter One

PRESENT DAY

I am running again and being chased. Bullets are flying past me as I try to outrun what's behind me. Ducking lower on my horse, not a horse I recognize so clearly, one I stole, I dig my heels in again spurring it on faster.

Glancing over my shoulder, I see them. Three riders dark against the night we are flying through. I can't see their faces but something tells me if I don't outrun them, I'm not going to be alive for much longer.

The horse stumbles and I'm thrown from the saddle. I slide down a hillside, branches and rocks tearing up my skin as I reach for anything to stop myself. Finally stopping, I look back up to see the three riders above me still on their horses.

"You never were a good rider unless it was on Tex," one of them says, the voice sounding too familiar.

"Too bad Tex is dead." Another chuckles.

I feel the dread form in the pit of my stomach, bile threatening to make its way up. Tex couldn't be dead, I wouldn't know what to do without him. I pull myself up and onto my feet, if this is the end, I will face these assholes like I faced everything else.

"You're lying!" I snap.

"Ah, she speaks," the first one says and I squint in the dark. "It's about time."

"Now, you're going to tell us where you stashed all that gold and we're going to kill you," the third says, a glint of silver flashing in their hand.

"Don't you mean *or* you'll kill me?" I reply.

"Oh no, we *are* going to kill you. It's what you deserve after leaving us behind. Do you know how long we stayed in jail after that heist?" the first one says.

"Ten months and then they killed us," the second chimes in.

"If they killed you, how can you be here?" I ask.

The third one snickers before lighting a match. I can see his face for only a moment, but that bile rises higher in my throat. His skin is peeling off his face, bone exposed to the light of the match. When he inhales the cigarette he had just lit, the amber glow lights the features of the one next to him. Bone exposed, teeth no longer hidden behind lips, and flesh hanging from his jaw.

They all laugh again, together this time, before I realize who I am staring at. Flynn, Holt, and Virgil have chased me down to kill me and are not alive anymore. What the hell am I looking at and talking to, then? Before I can ask another question, Virgil drops the cigarette in the grass beside him and it quickly catches flame.

They move toward me and as I turn to run I realize I'm surrounded, but not by anything I have ever seen before. People, at least they look sorta like people, stand everywhere around me in all conditions, but not one of them looks to be alive anymore. The panic sets in and I quickly look for a way out before a hand that's more bone than skin grabs the back of my neck and yanks my head back.

Looking up into what is left of Flynn's face, I feel my heart race. It looks like that body I had seen at the fair when I was younger. An exhibit from Egypt, a mummy. Flynn smiles at me, at least I think he tried to, before tightening his hold on my neck making me cry out.

"Time to die, Wren. It's your punishment for leaving us behind," he all but hisses into my face.

I wake up with a start, bolting upright, covered in sweat, my heart beating so fast I'm sure it will break free from my chest. I drag my hands down my face, wiping some of the sweat off before tossing the blankets off me. Sitting at the edge of the bed, I rest my head in my hands, breathing deeply till my heart calms again. There will be no going back to sleep after that one.

Looking out the window, I see the pink tinted sky. It's morning, but just barely. Tex will be awake and looking for breakfast. After that nightmare, I need a bath. I throw on clothes quickly before gathering what I will need at the bathhouse and throwing them into my bag. Tugging on my boots, I walk out the side door to see Tex staring at me.

"Yeah, yeah. I had another nightmare. I don't want to hear it from you," I say, patting his head before dropping some hay into his feeder. "I'm going to the bathhouse and then to work. Don't get into trouble while I'm gone."

Tex ignores me, but that's just because I fed him. Climbing the steps back inside, I grab my satchel and cross the floor to the front door. Pulling it closed behind me, I don't bother to lock it, no one is going to go through my house. I make my way through the town as it still sleeps and to the bathhouse. I'll have a nice hot bath and then some breakfast at the saloon before heading to work.

Stepping out into the morning sun, I stretch my arms over my head. It's already too damn hot for the coat I'm wearing, but it covers the weapons I keep on me at all times. Lifting my hand, I shade my eyes as I look down the street. People will be out soon enough, everyone wanting to get their things for the day before noon, when it's too bloody hot to do anything.

Starting down the road, I wave good morning to those I pass and nod my head to others. The silver star on the loop of my belt shows anyone who might not know who I am, what position I am in. Not that we get many newcomers in town. Since I arrived, we have had a total of ten and only four of them stayed to settle down. The joys of being a town near a mining camp.

I make my way to the sheriff's office, pushing open the door and closing it behind me just as quickly. There's one person in a cell, our town drunk, if he wasn't there it was because I pulled him off one of the saloon girls and sent him on his way with a firm threat of violence. I settle in the chair at the desk with a heavy sigh.

When I arrived in Skullpass, I had intended to spend a short while here. Just long enough to heal from my injury and make sure the heat was off me. What had happened was I decided I liked who I was here. So, when I was healed up, I looked for some more permanent housing. The sheriff had shown me a small house that had a corral attached to it for Tex. It wasn't for rent, it was for sale, which meant I would have to put down roots there.

I had looked at the house and noted all the things that needed to be fixed. The sheriff followed me through, talking about who had lived there before. A husband and wife, they decided they couldn't make it there anymore and had moved back to a larger city where the wife was from. The sheriff watched me walk the space looking around before letting me know there were several men in town who could help fix it up.

Smiling at him, I informed him that I wasn't afraid of some hard work and could handle most of the repairs myself. I just needed him to tell me where to get the materials. The sheriff had smiled at me and I wasn't sure I liked it.

"Sounds like you might be thinking about staying around for a while," he said.

"I think I might try to stay in one place for more than a month. I came into some money before getting into that fight with those men I was telling you about. Might be nice to put that money to good use and set down some roots for a bit." I rested my hands on my hips before giving the house a once over again. "Who do I talk to about making the purchase?"

The sheriff had taken me down the main road to the bank where I put the down payment on the house. The banker, a stuffy-looking old man with more hair on his face than his head, had lifted a brow at me.

"You sure you're going to be able to afford the rest?" he asks, giving me a once over look.

"Don't worry about it. I have my money stored away, I'll bring the rest down tomorrow." I signed my name on the papers and snatched the key to the house from him. "Have a nice day."

That was five years ago, and I haven't left yet. I am starting to like it here. The people are friendly and no one knows who I was before I showed up that night. My face is new and fresh to them, it had been covered in dirt and I was bloody that first night, but I was new. Something every town needed, new people to keep it growing.

I hear the groan from the cell and know our regular has woken up. The thump that follows tells me at some point during the night, he got onto the top bunk. I drop my feet to the floor from where they had been resting on the edge of my desk and make my way to the bars.

"Well, good morning, Hank. How are we feeling this morning?" I ask, cheerfully.

He groans and puts a hand to his head. "Too loud. Too happy. Too early."

"Ah come on, Hank. It's a beautiful day and you have

work to do. My corral isn't going to fix itself after your little incident. Unless you'd like to serve your time here with me every day, happy and chipper." I smile down at him.

"Good Lord, no." He pushes to his feet, dusting off his backside before looking at me. "Let me out. I'll go get my tools and have your corral fixed before nightfall."

"That's what I thought." I snatch the keys off the wall and unlock the cell door, letting it swing wide.

"I'll never understand how a woman your size can handle every issue this town has," Hank mumbles as he stumbles toward the door.

"Make sure that corral is straight, Hank! No leaning. Tex won't be happy," I call as he pulls the door open and steps out.

His one-handed wave tells me he heard me, but I am still sure it would lean just a little bit. Hank's little incident had come at the cost of a bruised-up side for him. He was riding his horse home, drunk one night, and his horse decided to take him for a ride right through my corral. Tex was pissed and kicked Hank in the side when he tried to use him to get up. Tex was in the right, Hank's horse went home without him, and Hank ended up in my cell for three days.

I cross the room, leaving the cell door open to lean against the door frame. I watch as the town comes alive. People appearing out of nowhere. Adeline making her way to the saloon down the street, probably to make sure nothing was damaged overnight. Mrs. Keen and her group of tiny offspring making their way toward the general store. By the looks of it, little Jimmy is in trouble again, his mother's grip on his hand is firm.

I had learned everyone's name in town. Who they were related to and how they came to be in Skullpass. It is a large town, but it's my job to know everyone, and I am sure to find out everything. Whatever it takes to keep this town safe from what lays outside it. It's bad enough we have the miners come through here every week. I'm not sure the town can handle any threat bigger than that.

So, when I see Levi heading toward me at a sprint, I know something is wrong. He stops at the bottom of the steps, bent over with his hands on his knees, panting heavily. He had run from his post just outside of town, that didn't seem like a good thing.

"What happened, Levi?" I ask calmly.

"Outside of town... I could see them... three of them... riding from the west." He pauses, taking a deep breath before standing upright again. "I think we have newcomers coming and I'm not sure they are friendly. They are moving fast, Sheriff Wren, faster than I have seen anyone in a long time."

Shit, I thought to myself. "Back to your post, Levi. I'll be out there shortly. Keep out of sight. Don't stop them, don't greet them, just watch. You understand me?"

"Yes, ma'am." Levi nods before turning to sprint back down the road.

What are the odds that it's them? It couldn't be them, could it? A cold shiver runs down my spine as I turn back into the office. Pulling the door closed, I tug my hat down on my head before starting down the street.

Only one way to find out.

Chapter Two

Out in the middle of town, I find the strangers are still on the edge of town. I start rushing people into the stores and out of the road in case the bullets start flying.

The three men just stop right before the main building starts in town. All of them lingering there, taunting me. I stand my ground, not budging from my position. All the townfolk are out of harm's way for the time being. Levi is out of earshot. Thankfully, he listened to me for once. When I strolled into town Levi was a lost puppy always following me around. Now he looks at me like he's a lovesick puppy but I've only ever seen him as a little brother.

His father gave me this badge, knowing his son wasn't ready to fill his shoes. The men don't move. With the sun beating down on me, I'm not sure how much longer I'll be able to stand here. If I was on Tex, I could wait them out all day. Edgar joins me after about ten minutes, his fingers are itching to pull one of his guns.

"How about you get your dumb ass back up to safety where I had you," I quip, glaring at him.

"Now, now, Sheriff Wren, I can't let you have all the fun, can I?" he scoffs.

"I can just put a bullet in your ass right now if you'd like," I tell him, locking my eyes to his deep-brown ones, his jet-black hair slicked back under his cowboy hat. It peeks out the bottom of his hat. Edgar is as good with his gun as he is with his dick. He's not half bad to look at, but lacks it in personality, too.

"Why are you always so stubborn, Wren?" he questions me.

"It's kept me alive this long. So, why change a good thing?" I smirk. "Move your ass before I move it for you."

"How come we can't stand with you, Sheriff?" a gruff, raspy voice states behind me.

"Buck, who let you off the leash?" I growl at him. This man is sexy as hell but I'll never let on to that.

"It's not a short one. Plus, I thought three on three would be best."

"Well, you thought wrong," I inform him. "If you want a spot in my jail cell then you can stand next to me. If you'd rather not, I suggest you heed my warning and get back to the saloon."

Adeline pops her head out of the saloon doors, seeing the two men with me, she's about to beeline it over to us. I just shake my head and she stops in her tracks. At least Adeline listens. If these two men don't move, I'll just shoot them myself. They pay me to do a job in this town, the people need to let me do it.

As soon as I bring my attention back to the three strangers they vanish.

"Anyone have eyes on them?" I yell out.

No one speaks out. They had just been there and now they're gone. Someone had to see where they rode off to. Am I still dreaming? I pinch my arm to see if it hurts.

"Fuck," flies from my lips.

"Why did you do that?" Buck laughs.

"I was hoping this was a dream. How could all three of them just disappear into thin air?" I'm so confused

"Maybe they realized this wasn't the town for them," Edgar suggests with a shrug.

"There was no mistake. Something feels off about the whole thing," I tell them. "I'm going to need you both to help keep an eye out to see if they come back. I want to be notified of anything out of the ordinary."

"You know we have other jobs, right?" Edgar interjects, letting out a little laugh.

"As of right now, you have all been deputized. It is my right to do so. This town could be under attack at any moment and we need to be ready, boys."

With that, I tell them to patrol the outskirts of town, only coming to find me if they find anything out of the ordinary. I'm off to let Levi know the same.

"What kind of job does Buck really have?" I mumble to myself. "He's just a hired gun. Fastest gunslinger I've seen besides me."

Adeline can watch The Golden Gait saloon for Edgar, he's a shitty owner and bartender anyway. The men go to see Adie, she's way better at both. Time to go look for Levi's normal spots to see if he's hiding there still. His favorite spot is above the wash house. Levi loves to watch the womens' bath; every now and again, I give him a little extra show. Not that he can see much from his perch.

"Levi, is your ass up there?" I call once I've made it to the bath house.

It's quiet, not a peep. He must be with Tex and that scoundrel who's fixing the corral. Levi is probably helping himself to my food. That boy doesn't know how to cook, plus he spends all his money on alcohol and bullets. That boy can't hit the broadside of a barn, he needs all the practice he can get. On the walk to my place, I keep my eyes peeled for the strangers. Nothing out of the ordinary, Rufus is in the alley throwing up. If I had more time, he'd go in the jail cell for the night. Not the normal town drunk, but a good stand once a week.

"Rufus, go home," I call to him, "or so help me when I come back, I'll lock you up."

He nods quickly before stumbling off. My home is right around the corner. Tex whinnies as he sees me, I try to hush him in case the desperados are close by. I round the corner to the backside of the corral and run smack into Levi.

"What the hell are you doing here?" I almost scream at him.

"I was following them," he whispers. "They seemed to vanish into thin air."

By the looks of him, he's seen a ghost, or three. His skin is paler than I've ever seen. If I hadn't seen it with my own eyes I'd have called him a liar, but how can grown men vanish so quickly.

"I've got Edgar and Buck keeping lookout," I explain to him. "I need you to do the same. If they come back we need to be ready. I have a bad feeling."

"Tex was telling on the town drunk, he was napping on the job. He's back at working on the corral now. I gave him the right motivation."

I laugh, "Good thing you aren't me. I would have punched him in the gut to wake him up."

"Yeah, I told him that you'd probably be back soon to check on him, he jumped up like lightning and got right back to work."

"That lazy ass." I grind my teeth. "If he's not done fixing the mess he made he can rot in the jail cell. Then I'll just have to fix it myself."

"What do you know about fixing a barn?" Levi questions me.

"Not a damn thing but I'm sure I can do better than someone sleeping on the job."

I give Levi his mission, he needs to go to the bath house and get back to that perch for now. I'll rustle him up some food as well as Edgar and Buck. I'd like to walk the edge of the town, but I'm sure they are long gone. Hopefully, for good.

They didn't seem like the normal miners that come to town. No wagons with them, only on horses. Where are their families? Most young men come with their fathers, trying to strike it rich for their loved ones. The rest of the family soon to follow.

The air around the town is still ominous, everyone is too quiet. With no noise, it is a bit easier for me to find anything out of the normal. I mount Tex as he looks as if he needs some fresh air; once Levi is in the lookout we make way. Riding Tex makes it a lot faster but damn if Buck and Edgar were not where I told them to be. It will be their hides when I get ahold of them.

I steer Tex straight for the Golden Gait, dismounting and rushing through the doors. There sits Buck with a beer in hand and Mabel in his lap giggling—probably at one of his lame jokes. I pull my gun out aiming for his mug. As I pull the trigger the mug Buck's holding explodes, glass goes flying everywhere. There's no way that could have made contact, yet Mabel shoots up with a scream, scrabbling to get away from Buck, as he jumps up, too. I move toward him, gun still drawn.

"Have you lost your mind, Wren?" Buck bellows over me, not backing down even though my gun's out.

"When I tell you to do something, you will do it," I tell him in a low growl.

"No man," he chuckles. "Or woman, is the boss of me."

"That is a joke. You are a gun for hire," I boast, giving him a glare. "You will do anything for money. Everyone is your boss, asshole. So, go keep watch like I said and I'll bring you dinner in a bit."

He swallows hard and just shakes his head. I point to the door with the hand that's free and he runs out without a word. My attention turns to Edgar, he's behind the bar hitting on Adie as she pours a drink for a customer. My feet move right to him, my gun points in his face.

"Of all the lowlife people I've met, I didn't think you'd be a worthless, no good piece of crap that doesn't listen when the law tells them to do something." My rage has overtaken me. Most days, I can suck it down but today has sent me over the top. "You yellow belly shit bag. Let's go. Maybe a couple days in the slammer will make you think twice before you disobey a direct order from me."

Edgar is shaken by my words, as am I. I've let too much slide in the past, but no more. I'm going to make up for my sins and the sins of others. My gun never leaves being trained on Edgar as we make our way over to the jailhouse. No words are exchanged between us, I'm done with his bullshit for today. He just gets in the cell, no questions asked.

"I fucking get you needed to show you are a big, bad man," I tell him as I lock the door behind him. "But today is different. This wasn't like our normal visitors. The three strangers had a bad aura over them."

"What do you mean aura? You a witch or something?"

"Shut the hell up!" I yell at him. "You didn't feel it just by looking at them?"

Chapter Three

The way Edgar looks at me makes me wonder if I had imagined it. He leans forward, his arms resting on the bars of the cell.

"Wren, there was nothing outta the normal about those men. Other than they picked the wrong town to come to," Edgar says.

I step back from the bars before turning on my heel toward the door to the office. Slamming it hard behind me, it only slightly muffles the sounds coming from behind me as Edgar yells for me. Something is wrong and whatever it is, I am going to figure it out.

I walk back toward the Golden Gait where Tex is still patiently waiting outside the doors for me. Tex is the only man I can count on, it doesn't matter he's a horse, he understands more than most do when it comes to me.

I pat his shoulder as I walk by, returning to the Golden Gait. Pushing open the doors, I walk in to find Mabel standing at the counter talking to Adie. The saloon quiets a bit as I make my way across the floor to the bar where Adie waits.

"You okay, Wren? You seem more on edge than normal." Adie reaches behind her for a bottle.

"I'm okay. Those visitors were unexpected on the outside of town, so I told Edgar and Buck to take up lookouts." I shake my head as Adie raises the bottle. "I don't ask much from them but something about those men seemed wrong. Then I find them in here messin' about." I motion to Mabel before shooting a glare her way. "I know Buck likes to fuck around with Mabel but damn it all, when I tell him to do something, I shouldn't have to go searchin' for him!"

"Jealous, Wren?" Mabel smirks at me.

"Mabel, you'd have to have something for me to be jealous of." I turn to face her. "You want to be the one I send out to those men if they show again?"

Mabel visibly pales. "You wouldn't."

"No, I wouldn't. But that's because I'm protecting this town and everyone in it, and that includes your sorry ass." I can feel that heat spiking in my veins again. "So, next time, maybe ask what Buck is supposed to be doing, rather than getting an easy fuck from him!"

Mabel stands slowly from where she had been leaning on the counter. She exchanges a look with Adie before making her way across the saloon toward a table of poker players. I rub a hand over my face, feeling the sweat building below the rim of my hat. Geez, it is fucking hot.

"That wasn't like you, Wren," Adie says, pouring a shot and sliding it down the bar top toward a patron.

"She's pissing me off, Adie. I do my best to keep the town safe and that's what she has to say to me?" I reply, watching Adie replace the bottle.

"She's young. She doesn't have the world experience that we do." Adie glances up at me before wiping the bartop down with a rag. "Maybe you should pay a visit to the doc. You don't look so good."

"I'm fine, Adie. Just these men pissing me off." Even as the words leave my lips, I know they are wrong.

"Here." Adie pushes a glass toward me and I look at her. "It's water. I'm gonna go see about getting the boys some dinner for you to take to them."

"I didn't say nothin' about dinner for them," I say, picking up the glass.

Adie grins at me as she walks down the back side of the bar. "You didn't have to."

Raising the glass to my lips I intend to take a little sip of the water to appease Adie. I'm not scared of her, but if I would protect anyone in town more than the others, it would be Adie. She is the one to patch me up without question. She took me in and gave me what I needed without pressing for information. Adie is the one who I need in town and not just for the liquor she pours.

The water touches my tongue and that small sip I had intended turns into me draining the glass. I swear it was full one second, and the next, it was empty. I set the empty glass on the bartop before turning my head to scan the room. The volume around me had increased while I talked to Adie. The poker table in the corner is more heated than the rest of the room, so my eyes linger there watching the men.

Some are people who live in town, others are visiting miners just passing through for a good time and some rest. Most are calm enough, but every so often, we get a rowdy bunch that need to be reminded they are only visitors. And they do not know how to react when I show up.

I watch as one of the men slams his cards onto the table with more force than necessary, my eyes tracking Mabel as she backs away from him. Sighing, I turn my back to the bar so I can give the table my complete attention. Things are going to go badly real quick if that man doesn't settle down.

The dealer spins the cards across the table and I watch the

man's face darken with each card he picks up. I feel my fingers twitch, eager to have a weapon in my hand when things go sideways, which they are quickly moving toward. He tosses down two cards when the rest of the table does and picks up his new cards.

I push off the bar as I see his face change. Mabel glances at me before backing into a nearby corner. The man is barely to his feet when I make it to him. Gun in hand, I have it raised to his head before he is able to move.

"I would strongly recommend thinking twice before doing what I think you were about to do," I mutter darkly.

His eyes flicker to the side, taking in the gun aimed at him as well as the star that glistens on my hip. He has a split second to make a decision, but he takes longer than my patience will allow. Using my thumb I pull the hammer back, the gun making the unmistakable sound as the cylinder rotates into place.

Slowly, he raises his hands in surrender and I pull the gun back the smallest of spaces.

"I suggest you take whatever money you have left and leave. We don't take kindly to people causing trouble in this town," I say, feeling the eyes around me.

"Yes, ma'am," he whispers gruffly, before reaching down and picking up the small pile of money in front of where he had sat.

I keep the gun aimed at him as he pushes the chair in and makes his way quickly to the doors, pushing through before breaking into a run. Slowly releasing the hammer, I holster my gun before turning back to the bar where Adeline is standing, now holding two pans.

Crossing to the bar again, I reach for the pans only to have Adeline pull them back. I look at her and she squints at me for a second before setting them down and refilling the glass again.

I sigh heavily before draining the glass again, this time under Adeline's watchful gaze.

"Happy?" I ask, setting the empty glass down.

"No. I want you to go see the doc. Somethin ain't right with you, Wren." She shakes her head.

"I'm fine. I need to take the boys dinner and figure out what in the hell is happening around here," I say, reaching for the pans again.

"No," Adeline replies, setting the pans behind her.

"No?" I question, actually confused by her firm tone.

"I'll have one of the boys take the dinner. You go see the doc." She pins me with a look that says she isn't budging about it. "Right now."

I lick my dry lips before giving into her demand. I nod to her once before heading for the door. She's right, something is off with me, but I can't let anyone know. I shove the doors open before stomping down the stairs onto the street. Tex grunts, gaining my attention.

"Yeah, yeah. She yelled at me, too. Let's go," I mumble to Tex before swinging into the saddle.

The doctor is just down the road, but I'm not going to leave Tex behind while I go see the doc only to have him say I am fine. Tex trots down the road, seeming content with my decision. I slow him near a watering trough that is beneath a tree. Plenty of shade for him to wait in while I'm inside.

Tex lowers his head to the water as I dismount and start toward the small building next to the doctor's house. He had built a small office not long ago so he didn't bring anything into the house with his family. I couldn't blame him.

I slow, seeing a familiar figure running toward me, hand on his hat keeping it in place, the other hand clutching a fluttering paper as he speeds toward me. It is never good when the telegraph operator sends his helper out with the message.

It could only mean something bad was happening.

Chapter Four

Logan comes running up to me, the paper almost flying out of his hand a couple times, but he makes it to me, breathless.

"This just came in from one of the bigger cities," Logan says, sucking in a deep breath.

As I take the paper from him, he runs right back from where he came. Looking at the telegraph in my hand, which reads:

New sickness- stop
From the water -stop
Coming from river Demon Hollow -stop

My stomach rumbles after reading that. I can feel the water I just drank wanting to come back up and I'm wanting it to. Our well water feeds from the same river. After dry heaving a couple times, nothing happens. It's back to see the doc, folding up the paper and keeping the information to myself for the time being. No, first I have to talk to Noah, he can't tell anyone about what came through. Just me, him, Logan, and the doc can know.

If and when this virus does hit us then I'll deal with the consequences. Hell, nothing ever happens here, so I'm sure this won't be anything new.

"Noah," I call out as I get close to the post office. Still sweating, my stomach starts to cramp. "Noah," I grunt as I bring my hand to my stomach.

Finally once I'm on the steps, Noah comes barreling out of the post.

"Wren, what's all the commotion?" he asks until he sees the state I'm in. "Let's get you to the clinic now."

There is urgency in his voice, as he throws my arm over his shoulder. Now spinning me around, back in the direction I just fucking came from.

"Look, you can't tell anyone about the telegraph," I grunt out between the pain shooting through my stomach. "We don't want people in hysterics over this, if there is nothing really here."

"Says the sheriff that's showing symptoms of sickness."

"I must've just eaten something that didn't agree with me," I manage to get out before I stop and throw up.

Noah jumps out of the way before it hits the ground. There is a splatter next to me; turning my head, I find Noah has started vomiting, too. My stomach feels so much better getting out whatever was making it rumble.

"Noah, you good?" I question him, bringing myself back into a standing position.

Noah moves around our mess and away from the smell. "Yeah, if I hear someone get sick, it makes me do the same."

"Good. I was scared for a moment. Unloading my stomach made me feel a ton better."

Noah gives me a look as he grabs me by the arm. "Wren, you aren't going to get out of seeing the doc that easily. You're still sweating like a stuck pig."

"Like you have room to say anything, your brow isn't doing you any favors," I tell him as I start for the clinic door.

"Just get your ass in there. If I feel a fever coming on, I'll go see him, too," Noah reassures me.

I look him dead in the eye before I turn the knob on the door "No one can know about the virus. No one."

Noah just nods and scurries away without a word.

"There's a bullet in your ass if you do!" I yell to him before heading in.

Doc Jed Jud sits behind his desk just about to nod off until I shut the door behind me a little harder than I needed to. He jumps a bit at the noise, popping his eyes open to see me walking toward him.

"Sheriff Wren, this is a nice surprise. I didn't see you come in," he says, standing up to greet me.

I let out a laugh, "Maybe you'd see better if you were awake when I walked in."

"I was just resting my eyes."

"If you say so," I say as I take a seat on the exam table.

Doc gets up and comes over to me, "Wren, you haven't been in here since you showed up shot all those years ago."

"Are you still on that? I could have handled that wound myself. Adeline is the one who brought you to my room. I was doing good dressing it."

"If I hadn't stepped in, infection might have started but it all worked out. What brings you in tonight?"

He brings me back to why I'm here.

"You know Ade, she thought I looked pale and sent me to my room. Aka to come see you," I explain to him. "Left my lunch on the sidewalk out front and I'm feeling so much better."

"Go home and get rest if you throw up any more. I'm going to give you some laudanum to help you sleep, and in case you start coughing from fever." Doc Jud hands me the bottle.

I shake my head, but he forces it in my hand. "I'm feeling much better."

He smiles, patting my hand and letting go. "Just in case."

"Oh, I almost forgot." I hand him the telegraph. "This just came in. Only me, you, and Noah know about this. Maybe Logan knows but let's keep it this way. We don't want the townsfolk up in a roar."

Doc gives me a look. "You don't think that's what you have, do you?"

"I promise you I'm fine. I must have eaten something that had soured my stomach."

"This won't come from my lips until you say." He nods as he goes back to his chair.

"Thank you, old man. Now finish that nap before you head for bed." I laugh to myself as I head out to collect Tex and head home.

Sleep does sound pretty good right about now. Between nightmares, strangers disappearing, and my stomach gurgles, sleep feels very welcoming. Tex whinnies at me when I exit the building.

"Oh you big lug, I'm fine," I tell him, grabbing his reins and turning him toward home. "It's time for some rest. Tomorrow feels like it's going to be a doozy."

My eyes pop open to Levi shaking me awake.

His voice is high pitched when he sees my eyes open.

"Wren, they're back. Them gentlemen are sitting on the edge of town again."

"Ugh, what?" His words just go through my head; I don't understand anything he's said.

Levi's out of breath this time telling me. "The ones from yesterday. Sitting on the outskirts of town."

I shoot up in bed. My head is spinning. Wow, the medicine Doc gave me hit me hard. Probably why I didn't have any dreams last night. Well, any I can remember.

"Go keep an eye on them. I'll be out shortly," I tell him as I sit up, swinging my legs over the side of my bed.

My boots hit the floor, I must've passed out as soon as I sat down. No time to change.

"Shit, where did I put Tex?" I mumble to myself as I get up to go grab him.

If I wasn't awake before, I am now. Those strangers aren't going to get away today. Stumbling out, I find Tex standing out front of my house, odd place for him to be. Thankfully, he's not pissed at me for just leaving him wherever. Most of the time he doesn't let me touch him if I don't take care of him. Tex could probably feel that I was off last night, so he gave me a pass.

After mounting him, I ride to the middle of town, holding the reins a bit tighter than normal. The laudanum still feels like it has a bit of a hold on me but I feel shit-ton better than last night.

Back in the middle of town, the men sit in the same spot they were yesterday. I know that they weren't just in my head yesterday.

Why do they just sit there doing nothing?

Must be doing it just to get in my head. Today, I'm going to find out what these assholes want.

"Levi," I call as he tries to sneak past me. Not sure what he is thinking but he's not that bright. "Get your ass over here."

Off the porch and on to the road he scurries right over to me. Tex greets him with a whinny.

He looks up to me. "What you need, Sheriff?"

"Please go release the prisoner. I might need him out here to help. And if you see Buck tell him to get the fuck out here."

Levi nods and rushes toward the sheriff's office. My eyes are trained on the mysterious men that haven't budged. The crowd is starting to gather as they did yesterday. I'm not going to just stay here like I did yesterday. Adie comes out of the Golden Gait as I start riding toward the shadows. The closer I get, the clearer the face of the man becomes. My heart skips a beat as I see who is sitting in front of me.

"Well, well, looky who we have here, boys," Virgil says as he shows no emotion.

Holt lets out a cough before he speaks. "She left us for dead."

"No, I told you to follow me. I know I did," I try to explain but they aren't wanting to listen to me.

Flynn puts his two cents in. "You just grabbed all the money you could get your hands on and disappeared into the sunset."

"You have it all wrong. Tex and I barely made it out of there with our lives. I have the scars to prove it," I say but they are still just glaring at me.

Virgil coughs, too, sweat rolling off his forehead. "Do you know how long it took us to find you?"

"I'm guessing until now." I giggle at the wrong time.

"Where is the money?" Holt screams at me.

I'm almost at a loss for words at him demanding my part of the score. "Are you kidding me? You came here for money? Why would you think I'd have any of it left? You could just do another job. The three of you should have been set from the last one we did together."

"No, Wren, we weren't. When we opened those bags they

were only half full," Holt tells me. "But I know I saw her stuff one to the brim, so you must have gotten that one."

"How is that my fault? It was crazy in there. All of us are lucky to be alive. But mine wasn't overflowing," I lie to him, I can feel the anger rising in my voice, knowing I need to pull back before they do something stupid. Or I do. "I don't have any left. I had to take a job just to get by."

I flash off my badge. All three of them are shocked to see it. It's not something I'd ever thought I'd do. I thought to avoid the law was to stay on the run, but it was to become one of them.

"How could you become a traitor?" Flynn sounds so betrayed.

"I had to find some work and the best way to stay hidden was to become the law," I tell them, my brain is trying to think of a way to get rid of them. "So, since I don't have what you're looking for, I'm going to have to ask you to head off to another town."

"Not going to happen, Wren," Virgil informs me. "We are going to stay here till we get what we are owed."

Chapter Five

Staring at him in disbelief, my eyes flicker to Virgil as he coughs again. The words of the telegraph come back to me. Tex shifts beneath me, clearly not trusting the men in front of us, or maybe he knows something I don't.

"Tell ya what, why don't you come to the Golden Gait? I'll have Adeline set you boys up in a room and we can talk over something to eat. I'm sure you could use a drink." If talking sense into them wouldn't work, maybe offering them some hospitality would.

Holt bows over the pommel of his saddle, the horn digging into his chest as another coughing fit overcomes him. He spits on the ground and I can see the sweat rolling off of his head in heavy lines now. I could only hope that Virgil would take the bait and let me get them to the Golden Gait.

"Holt looks like he could use some rest and a drink. What do you say, Holt?" I turn my attention to Holt as he rights himself in the saddle again.

Holt lifts his eyes to my face and it seems like he isn't seeing me at all, for a brief second. Flynn seems to be the only one that isn't coughing or pouring sweat like he was working in the fields. Possibly the only one who might be thinking clearly.

"What do you say, Flynn? For old time's sake." I turn my eyes to him, hoping he will be able to convince the others to come with me.

Flynn's eyebrows move the tiniest bit, acknowledging that I had an idea, before looking at Virgil who I can swear is sweating even more now. My heart beats faster as I wait for them to make a decision. Then, from the corner of my eye, I spot Edgar and Buck squatting behind a low wall. I keep my eyes on the trio in front of me though, not giving them away.

"Virgil, I think we should stay, at least for the night." Flynn, I notice, doesn't lean in when talking to Virgil. "We can get a night's rest in a room with a bed, have a good meal, drink till we are full, and not have to pay a dime." Flynn cocks his chin in my direction. "Wren here, will take care of everything. It's the least she can do after all the trouble she has caused."

It takes a lot for me not to yell at him for the last part, but he's working in my favor, so I bite my tongue while I watch Virgil roll the idea around. Virgil leans forward, resting his forearm on the pommel of his saddle.

"You can get us each a room? I ain't sharing with no one," Virgil replies.

"I'm sure Adeline has rooms available," I say.

"Then we stay the night." Virgil straightens up in the saddle before locking eyes with me. "Tomorrow, you will give us the money or there will be trouble."

There's no use arguing with him. Clearly, Virgil has only one thought on his mind and it's the gold that he is sure I still have. The money he swears I had stolen from them. We all had a bag in hand. It isn't my fault if they squandered it on liquor and women, while I was laid up trying to heal and deciding to lay low to take the heat off myself.

I don't agree to the last part, but I do give him a small nod of my head before turning Tex and allowing them to move their horses forward. I fall into line at the end next to Flynn, whose gaze flickers to the low wall where Edgar and Buck are still watching. I motion with my hand toward them to stay down, knowing they won't move until I am clear with the gang.

Virgil makes a few vulgar comments while we ride down the main street. A few regarding the newlywed couple that had moved to town not long ago and how the wife looks pretty unhappy. She doesn't, but I don't say anything either, just give the couple a nod of my head and they move along faster. Holt isn't far behind Virgil, as always, making a comment about how shitty the town looks.

I take a calming breath as we make it to the Golden Gait and I dismount Tex. Flynn swings down beside me and we bump into each other.

Memories rise with the touch. Late nights under the stars, sleeping out in the open. Virgil and Holt drunk off their asses, snoring so loud they could keep anything away from us. Flynn and I talkin' about where we came from, what we wanted in life. Flynn leaning toward me while I watched in disbelief. His lips brushing across mine, not quite tentatively but not completely sure either. One kiss led to another and we spent too much time at night under those stars stealing kisses and dreaming of the future that we both knew would never happen.

I take a step back, grabbing the reins from the saddle and tossing them over the hitching post. Flynn clears his throat before doing the same thing as I make my way around Tex to see Virgil stumbling off his horse and hitting the ground hard. Holt is attempting to dismount as well and failing. It's like they have no control over their bodies.

Holt thumps to the ground after the failed dismount and slowly makes his way onto his feet. Virgil is dusting off his hands when Holt stops next to him. I eye them both before turning and making my way into the Golden Gait, letting the doors swing behind me.

Adeline is standing behind the bar pouring a drink. When she looks up and sees me, she starts to smile. But the men behind me wipe the smile from her lips before it can form. I lean on the bar top as Adeline glances at the three of them before turning her eyes back on me.

"What can I do for ya, Sheriff?" she asks, wiping the bar down with her ever-present rag.

"Think I can snag a couple rooms for the boys here, Adeline? They need a good night's rest and a decent meal before moving on tomorrow," I reply, not dropping my gaze from hers.

"I'm sure we have a couple rooms on the second floor. Can I get the names to sign them in?" Adeline asks.

Before Virgil can say anything I speak up, cutting him off. "Just put my name, for all three. I'll handle the costs."

Adeline glances at the trio before looking at me and shrugging her shoulders. "Suit yourself, Sheriff."

Turning around she pulls three keys off the board next to the bar wall before handing them to me. "Thank ya much, Adeline. I'm gonna show them to the rooms and get them to the bathhouse before getting some food in them. Can ya help with that?"

Finally, Adeline smiles a little at me. "I sure can, Sheriff. I'll see what we can get together for them."

With that, Adeline turns on her heels and moves behind the bar toward the back room. I take a second before turning to the trio and motioning them toward the stairs. I follow behind as Virgil and Holt mount the stairs first, coughing the entire way. Flynn hangs back a moment, taking the stairs beside me.

I hand them each a key and show them their room, before

telling them to meet me downstairs in five to go to the bathhouse. I retreat down the stairs, sweat settling between my shoulders as I hit the floor and looked for Adeline. As if she has been summoned, she appears from behind the door to the back room again.

"Who are those men, Wren?" Adeline whispers.

"Adeline, those are mistakes from my past that have caught up to me." I glance up the stairs making sure none of them have reappeared. "I think they are sick. I need to help them sleep, if you understand."

"Oh, I understand. I've handled it." Adeline shakes her head. "I don't know much about your past, Wren, but those three look like trouble."

"They are trouble, Adeline, which is why I am trying to get them out of here as soon as possible." I hear a door close above us and step back from Adeline. "Stay away from them, Adeline. I will handle them."

Adeline's eyes widen a little but she nods once before heading to the bar again to handle the customers. At the top of the stairs, Flynn begins making his way down and I can't help but notice that even under that dirty face, he's still handsome. I frown for a second before shaking my head. Nope, that is not allowed. I'm trying to get rid of them, not keep them. Well, maybe just one.

"Virgil and Holt will be down in a sec," Flynn says, reaching the bottom stair. "Which gives us a second for me to ask, what in the fuck are you doing here? And as a member of the law? Are you out of your mind?"

"You have no idea what happened to me," I hiss at him. "You don't know what I went through, what lies I had to tell to survive here."

Flynn flinches a little, like I had physically struck him. "You're right. I have no idea what happened, because you abandoned us!"

"I didn't..." I take a deep breath hearing Virgil and Holt at the top of the stairs. "We'll finish this later."

"Ya, damn right we will," Flynn mutters before turning around.

Virgil and Holt reach the bottom of the stairs and I start for the door again, pausing outside long enough for them to grab their saddles and bags, before they follow me to the bathhouse. Taking the steps two at a time, I look back to see Virgil and Holt both staring up the stairs at me. Their faces are red and their breathing seems labored.

"Virgil, ya alright?" I call down, forcing him to look at me.

"I'm tired, not old. Give me a second," he snaps at me.

Flynn climbs the stairs to the top and waits beside me. Virgil and Holt start up the stairs again, complaining about the heat and how a cold bath would do them wonders. Stepping into the bathhouse, I smile at the owner, before letting him know that the boys are there to use the baths on my dime.

Just as with Adeline, he looks at me before asking if I am sure. I say I am and watch as the owner motions the three of them back.

"I'll be back at the Golden Gait when you are done. Take your time," I call as they follow him to the back.

Virgil and Holt don't so much as budge, but Flynn glances over his shoulder at me and nods. With any luck, Virgil and Holt will drown in the bath. Probably won't happen, but a girl can hope.

I sit at a table at the Golden Gait for well over an hour before one of them returns. Flynn wanders through the doors, looking cleaned and shaved, making my stomach feel like I have swallowed butterflies. Crossing the room, he takes the stairs two at a time, the saddle and bags across his shoulder, before disappearing into his room above.

Lifting the glass to my lips, I take a sip before setting it back down and running a finger around the top of the glass.

Virgil and Holt look like shit, which is unusual for them. They don't seem to be taking no for an answer, which isn't unusual for them. I rub my hand across my face. The new sickness, whatever it is, seems to be traveling fast. I have to do what I can to protect the town, even if that means playing nice with these dickheads.

The chair across from me scrapes across the floor, bringing me back from my thoughts. Flynn settles in the chair, stretching his long legs out in front of him. He cleans up nicely. I don't think I have seen him this clean in a while.

"Alright, Wren, spill it," he says, resting his elbows on the chair arms.

"Where do I start?" I reach for the glass, lifting it to my lips and draining it. "After the heist, when we were running away, I yelled for you boys to follow me. None of you did. I just figured we would meet up later. I waited for you, on the outskirts of town, for longer than I should've. I could have been caught. I decided that it was best for me to move on and maybe catch up with you all later." Adeline appears with another drink for me and a glass for Flynn. "Flynn, this is Adeline. She's the person who kept my ass in line for the doc to tend to me. Adeline, this is Flynn, he's a friend."

"Any friend of Wren's is a friend of mine." She plants a hand on her hip before pointing a finger at him. "Don't make me eat those words."

Flynn lifts the glass to her before taking a drink as Adeline wanders away. "Adeline take you in?"

"Sort of." I shrug before sitting forward. "I was shot in the heist. I barely stayed conscious long enough to make it here. Adeline didn't seem to care about what I said, only that I healed. After I healed, I decided laying low here wouldn't be a bad idea. Take some heat off of myself at least. The sheriff," I shook my head even as the smile tried to creep in. "He didn't trust me right away. I had to earn that trust, but I did eventually. He knew his son wouldn't be able to do the job. He said I was full of fire and drive, just what the sheriff needed." I take a sip of the drink before looking up at Flynn. "I've been the sheriff for the last four years. I've been keeping this town safe for that entire time. Nothing happens to anyone in town, nothing. The life I lived before is dead. No one here knows who I was before I arrived, no one cares. I do my job and I do it well, that's all they care about."

"What about us?" Flynn asks, twisting the glass between his long fingers.

"Us?" I ask, confusion making me frown.

"You, me, Virgil, and Holt. Us. What about us? Don't you care what happens to us?" Flynn asks, pinning me with a look.

I stare at him for a few seconds, the question making me pause to think about it.

Chapter Six

"'Us,' what the hell do you mean 'us?'" I ask, slamming my hands on the table. I can feel the heat rising in my chest, hopefully that fever's not getting worse. "There hasn't been an 'us' for five flipping years. I told you I've started a new life here. Come hell or high water, I won't give this up for anyone. Especially not for the likes of you all."

The warmth takes over my whole body.

"Wren?" Flynn's voice shakes, his eyes are wide.

"Spit it out, you know those two assholes will be here any moment," I try to rush him.

"Your... your eyes. I saw fire in them," he remarks.

I let out a grunt. "Because I'm pissed off."

"No, real flames. Like you were about to go up in smoke." Flynn's voice is still uneasy.

"I think you should go lay down. The heat of the day must have gotten to you. Or maybe Adeline made your drink stronger than you can handle." I tell him, now worried he might be coming down with the virus.

I know I told her to help make them sleepy but what did she put in his drink? Flynn is starting to see things.

Flynn laughs. "I've never met a drink that was too strong for me."

After his words, he stands—well tries. Flynn wobbles and sits right back down. Yup, the same guy I've always known, still can't handle any liquor. Going around to his side, I help lift him to his feet.

"Alright, Flynn, let's get you to your room before you make a fool of yourself," I whisper to him as I throw his arm over my shoulder.

He nods, giving me a smile. I've missed being this close to him. The warmth of his body next to mine is really bringing more memories flooding in. Shaking away any feelings I have for this man, I know my town is more important to protect than him.

Flynn is so out of it he can't even lift his leg to ascend the stairs. Out of the corner of my eye, I watch as Adeline comes over to me, probably seeing I'm having trouble with him.

"Maybe we should have Buck or Levi haul him up to his room," Adeline suggests.

"Those idiots would just get in the way," I mumble as we get him up a couple of stairs. "Now come on, Flynn, just a couple more steps till the top."

Flynn grunts as a reply, slowly lifting his leg to the next step but missing. He tries to stumble forward but we stop him from falling.

"I'll cut what I put in the other guys' drinks in half so they can make it to their rooms," Adeline tells me as we make it to the top.

"They can sleep on the ground outside for all I care. This one's the only one who's ever cared if I'd lived or died," I tell her as I dig for his key.

"Understood," is all that comes from Adeline.

I finally find his key as I hear my name being yelled from the saloon floor. Dammit. I was hoping they wouldn't have been back so soon.

"Can you keep those two distracted while I get this one settled in?" I ask as I open the door, shuffling him in.

Adeline nods, leaving Flynn to me. I drag his ass to the bed and he flops down face first as soon as I let go. I help him get his feet on the bed and roll over. As soon as he's face up, I take his boots off, he's always hated sleeping in them.

Flynn opens an eye and mumbles, "Thank you, Wren. I love you, darling."

His words make me freeze in my tracks. 'Love...' did he just say 'love?' Flynn has never uttered those words to me. I had a plan, a fucking plan. Now that's all out the window. Are these his true feelings or just whatever Adeline gave him?

A scream from the saloon floor brings me back to what I need to do. I toss the boots next to the door, quickly shutting it behind me.

As I hit the steps, I see Virgil's got Mabel in his lap. His arms are around her waist. But the thing that's out of the normal is he's latched onto her shoulder with his teeth. No matter how much she wiggles she can't get out of the hold of his teeth.

Virgil rips the flesh from her shoulder, chewing on what he has in his mouth. With no hesitation, I whip the pistol out, aiming right for Virgil's head.

I whisper as I'm about to pull the trigger, "At least you gave me a reason."

A shot rings out and Virgil goes limp in the chair. There's no time to look to see where it came from. I hop into action, running down the stairs.

Edgar makes it to Mabel before I do. His gun hasn't been holstered yet, with his free hand he's got a bar towel pressing down on the bite.

"What did I do?" His voice is wild with excitement and fear.

"Rush her to the doc, he'll get the bleeding stopped," I say, trying to be as cool as I can not to freak him out more.

Edgar nods his head yes, still not sure what just happened. I can't let the shock sink in as I turn my attention to Holt. If Virgil did that and Holt is showing the same symptoms... Virgil ripped right through Mabel's skin and was eating it like she was dinner.

Holt lets out a cough, causing Daisy to squeal. Daisy is still positioned on Holt's lap. After the sight she just saw, I don't know why she would still be anywhere near him.

I take Daisy by the hand, leading her off of his lap. "Thank you for keeping our guest company until I could get back to him."

"Oh, it was no trouble at all." She giggles with a wink to Holt.

"Holt, let's go," I tell him, pointing the pistol I never holstered at him. "Just to be on the safe side we're going to have you spend the night in my lovely jail cell. None of that funny stuff like Virgil."

Buck and Levi come running into the saloon.

Levi stops cold when he sees the body slumped in the chair. "Wow, Wren, you made quick work of this one."

"Wasn't me. Edgar got to him before I could," I explain as I move Holt closer to the door. "Please take him to the undertaker as I get this one to the sheriff's office. Oh and, boys, help Adeline clean up any mess."

Buck lets out a grunt in my direction. I just take that as a yes as I lead Holt to the jail. My gun now rests in the small of his back as we move faster. There are too many people around, I have to control him. Once in the office, Holt looks worried.

"Wren, you don't have to do this—" Holt begins.

"Do what?" I snap at him.

"Lock me up. You know I wouldn't hurt anyone." He's almost pleading.

"You saw the shit that went on in the Golden Gait. Virgil never ate anyone before, but there he was, chowing down!" I spit at him as I open the door, tossing him in. "I can't take any chances anyone else will get hurt. Now hand over your guns."

Holt is filled with rage now. "Come get them."

I smirk at him. "Or I can just shoot you where you stand and state you were coming after me like Virgil. You'd be dead and no one the wiser."

"Fine," he huffs as he unholsters his guns. Slowly handing them to me.

"Ah, don't forget about the hidden one," I tell him, as I move backward to set the two guns down on my desk without taking my eyes off him.

After a few moments, I hit the desk and lay the guns on it without looking. Holt is fishing out his last gun. I'm still not sure how he keeps it there or how it's comfortable.

"Here," Holt thrusts the gun at me.

I grab it and slam the door closed with my foot. Slipping his gun in my belt, I click the lock so he can't get out.

"Once Doc is done with Mabel, I'll have him come give you a look over. You really need that fever looked at," I say, finally feeling a sense of ease since he's behind bars.

"Five years really has changed you, Wren," he mutters as he sits on the bed. "I feel fine. Food would be nice or something to drink."

"After Doc sees you, I'll see about some grub." I sigh as I leave him to check on Mabel and get the doc to come here.

As soon as I get to the doc's, I find it is a sight. Mabel is a shell of herself, her eyes seem to be void of anything. Blood is splattered all around the chair Mabel is tied to. She's grunting and drooling as she tries to free herself to get to me; once I get closer, I see the drool is reddish-pink. Shock takes over as the realization is she's got blood dripping from her lips.

How does she already have the virus? What type of virus makes you hungry for human flesh? Where are the doc and Edgar?

I follow a trail of blood to a door leading to the Doc's house. My hand is a bit shaky as I grab the handle, swinging the door open. Doc is behind the door bleeding from his neck. His eyes look the same as Mabel's. He lunges forward at me, growling as he does. A strange sound I've never heard come from anyone before.

As I back up, I pull my gun, pointing it at him. Tears start welling up in my eyes. "Oh, Doc, what happened to you? Please, oh please, don't make me do this to you."

Doc just keeps coming for me; it's him or me. I'm not paying attention to my surroundings. With another lunge, I don't hesitate letting the gun fire. Hitting him in the right eye, he goes down like a sack of potatoes.

Just as I'm about to get my composure, I feel it, teeth clamping down on my forearm.

Chapter Seven

The scream is ripped from my chest as I feel the teeth tugging at the skin on my arm. Looking down as I bring my gun around, I see Noah latched onto my arm, tugging the skin.

"Damn it all!" I shout as I bring the gun to his head.

He doesn't so much as flinch as I pull the trigger. The back of his head explodes as his jaw finally lets go and his body drops to the floor. I look down at him, noticing the vacant look in his eyes before glancing up at Mabel. She's still struggling against the rope in the chair, growling and snapping at me.

The shiver runs over my entire body as I realize whatever sickness the telegram warned about has arrived and people are already falling ill. This isn't like anything I've ever seen before. It takes the person they were away so that it seems like they don't recognize anybody.

Crossing the room to Mabel, my arm bleeding and dripping down off my fingers, I stare down at her.

"I didn't mean what I said. You were a good person,

Mabel." Raising my gun, I feel the lump in my throat. "I'm sorry."

Her head drops the instant I pull the trigger and the bullet enters between those vacant eyes. Turning, I move toward the exam room, stepping over the doc's body. Pulling gauze from the cupboard, I wrap it around my forearm before looking back at the bodies.

Virgil bit into Mabel like she was a five-star dinner he was dying to have. Then Mabel became whatever that thing is. The blood around her must have been from the doc and he wasn't himself either. Noah laid on the floor, but didn't seem to have anything wrong with him. Except the telegram said it was in the water.

Looking down at my arm once more, I decide that if asked, I will say I cut myself. I need to save as many people as I can before whatever happened to them, happens to me. I feel my stomach curl at the thought, but I shove the feeling down.

I walk through the room making sure none of them are breathing anymore and close the door to the doc's office behind me. I stand on the small porch looking out toward town when I hear it.

Screams. Coming from all directions.

My feet are moving before my brain has time to put together what is happening. I sprint to the main road and stop in my tracks. My head's not able to comprehend what I am seeing.

Bodies litter the ground. Some young, some old. But each one I pass has those vacant eyes. Some people have flesh torn from their bodies, others seem more intact like Noah had been. Glancing down an alley, I see Logan staring down at old Mrs. Moore. He looks terrified but she is walking toward him slowly... and without her cane.

Turning down the alley I raise my gun and call out. "Logan, how does she look?"

"Like nothin' I have ever seen before," he calls back.

My voice drew Mrs. Moore's attention from Logan and toward me. Blood drips from her lips and those eyes are no longer kind and sweet. They are the eyes of someone who is dead, in more ways than one.

I pull the trigger and watch as she slumps to the ground. Logan skirts the wall around her, coming toward me. I hold the gun up until he stops and puts his hands up.

"I'm not sick, Wren," he whispers, his eyes wide with terror.

"Anyone tried to take a bite outta ya?" I ask.

"What? No!" Logan looks scared shitless.

"I just dropped Noah at the doc's. The doc and Mabel, too. They both had chunks taken from them, but not Noah," I say, not lowering my gun.

Logan's eyes go wider, I didn't think it was possible. "Water. He's been drinking water all day because it's so damn hot."

I let my gun dip a little, realizing what he said. We all drink the water, every single person. If whatever this is travels through the water, we are all infected.

"Why aren't you showing signs?" I ask suspiciously.

"I don't drink the water. I bring coffee from home," Logan replies.

"You use water to make coffee, you idiot," I mutter.

"But I don't feel like nothin' is wrong. Look!" He shoves his sleeves up to show me bare arms, same with his legs and finally pulls up his shirt to show no bites. "And I feel fine."

He doesn't look like the others and from the time Mabel was bit and turned to, whatever that thing was, didn't take long at all. If Logan was sick, he would show signs by now, wouldn't he? I lower my gun and see him draw a deep breath of relief.

"You gotta get outta here, Logan. I don't know what's

happenin' but it ain't good. Get home and lock yourself inside. Only let me in if I come," I tell him before starting to turn back to the street and the screams behind me.

"But, Wren," he starts and I look back to see him looking at my arm.

"I'm fine. Cut myself at the doc's office when I was trying to get away from the doc," I lie smoothly.

"Alright. You be careful." Logan watches as I turn my back to him again.

He would go home like I said. No one would want to be out after seeing that. Holstering my gun, my only thought is that I have to get back to the Golden Gait. I have to check on Adeline and...

"Shit!" I yell before starting to sprint toward the Golden Gait.

Flynn.

He was with Virgil and Holt. He could be sick and I left him at the Golden Gait with Adeline. If something happened to either of them... I won't let myself think about what I would have to do, all I can do is try to make sure they stay safe.

Sprinting to the Golden Gait is the easy part. Trying to ignore the sounds of the screams from all around me is the hard part. I dodge what looks like Mrs. Keen as three of her four kids chew on various parts of her. The bunch ignores me but it doesn't slip my notice that Little Jimmy is missing from the group.

A quick stop in my sprint allows me to avoid getting kicked by a rearing horse, who decides he isn't about to be anyone's meal, and launches a body across the street and through a window. I spare a quick glance around and swallow hard.

Main street is a mess of screams and bodies. Some trying to run, others makin' meals out of friends and family. I feel the wave of nausea hit me, causing my entire body to warm up.

Feels like that fever is making a return visit. I wipe the back of my hand across my brow before continuing toward the Golden Gait again.

I dip under a hitching post and climb onto the porch next door to the Golden Gait. Righting myself again, I draw my gun, turning around and seeing the bathhouse owner staggering towards me, his upper arm dripping blood from the stump where it used to be attached. His eyes look just like the rest. I can't remember how many bullets I have left. I reload the gun as fast as I can, spinning the barrel and snapping the six shooter back into place.

"For fuck's sake," I mutter, before pulling the trigger and watching him drop to the floor.

I can't hold it anymore. My stomach revolts and I lean over the railing next to me, emptying my stomach. Wasn't much there, but I felt better almost as soon as I did. The heat that had been trying to burn me up a few moments before was suddenly gone. Wiping my mouth with the back of my hand, I turn back to the doors of the Golden Gait and shove them open.

Only to be met with a shotgun shoved in my face.

Chapter Eight

My hands automatically go up with the gun still jammed in my face. Once my eyes focus, I find Adeline is the one holding the shotgun.

"It's me Wren!" I all but scream at her.

"Are you one of them?" her words are all but blurred together.

"If I was, I'd be trying to bite your ass," I say, grabbing the barrel and slowly lowering it.

"Sounds kinda kinky," I hear from behind Adeline. "Can we watch?"

Looking around Adeline to the right, I find Flynn is sitting there with a smile. How the heck is he even awake?

"Blow a hole in his ass would you?" I tell Adeline, pointing to Flynn. "He seems a little green around the gills."

"Woah, woah," Flynn retorts with a shit-eating grin on his face.

"You would smile with all this shit that's going on," I scold him.

"I'm still a bit high from whatever you drugged me with.

Can't even feel my face, let alone what it's doing," he says to me.

"No drugs…" I try to tiptoe around.

"Yeah, right," he lets out a low rumble.

Before I can get anything else out of my mouth, a blood-curdling scream comes from the front of the saloon. All eyes dart toward the front doors. Holt staggers in, bloody. I'm not sure it's his blood as no bites are visible. Why hasn't he turned like Virgil did? He had a fever when he entered town. But at this moment, that's not important.

"Holt, what the hell?" comes tumbling out of my mouth.

"The people out there… they," his breath is shallow as he sucks in air. "All…attacking…each other."

Holt finally gets all his words out as he takes the closest seat to himself.

"You know they can just walk in here," I tell him, trying not to laugh at his stupid ass. "Coming in here where the doors swing open and don't lock wasn't your brightest moment."

"Right now is not the time to fight," Daisy steps in my eyesight. "I'm scared shitless. Why are people eating each other?"

"That is the question," Buck's voice says from behind me.

I whirl around to him with my gun still drawn. "Where the hell did you come from?"

"Levi and I came in the back door, darling."

Not sure why he called me that but I'm relieved by Levi's face. He better just be bite free. I run over to him, pushing past Buck. Immediately, I grab his arms, checking for any marks. When I find none, I move on to his neck. Nothing. Starting to pull up his shirt to check is where he stops me.

"I've always dreamed you'd want to undress me, Wren, but not like this," Levi tells me as he shoves his shirt back down.

"Well, sorry to tell you kid, but this is the only way I'd ever do it." I wink at him, breathing a sigh of relief when I look away from him.

His father made me promise I'd look after him, way before he passed away. Boy, does that boy need all the help he can get. It's almost a full-time job just keeping his ass out of trouble.

Taking in a deep breath, I know I just need to tell them. "Noah got a telegraph from a neighboring town," I start, pacing the floor trying to think how to put it.

"Come out with it!" Holt's voice bellows.

I snap my attention to him. "Shut it so I can," I growl, glaring at him. "On the paper I was handed it said something about a virus that is spreading. To be on the lookout."

At this moment, I leave out that it has to do with the water. They don't need to know everything. It's my job to protect them, and that's what I'm going to do.

Adeline gets in my face. "How long?" her voice shakes. "How long have you known?"

"I didn't know this was going to happen," I say as calmly as possible. "How could I have known people would be eating each other? That was not in the memo."

"Ladies," Flynn finally stands, a little wobbly but he's on his feet. "Right now we need a plan. Feelings need to be set aside."

That's what I've been trying to do but everyone's emotions are on overload. My arm is throbbing and why is it so hot in here? They can't know I might have a fever.

"Everyone who's in here should stay put. Tex is out there and I'm not leaving him out in the open," I let them know, pacing again. "When I exit the building you need to block off all ways in."

"No, you can't go alone," Flynn interjects. "I'll go with you."

"You can hardly stand. How are you going to protect yourself let alone anyone else?" I spit his way.

"I'll just shoot both of them." He grins at me. "But you aren't going without me."

"Fine," I grit out through my teeth. "Let's go. Tex is running out of time."

The last place I remember leaving him is tied up in front of the saloon. In all the confusion of tonight, I don't remember seeing him still there. Tex is the one thing on this earth I can count on. He might be getting old but he's been the one constant thing in my life I can remember.

The doors swing behind me quickly, leaving me looking around at the shells of the people in this town. One thing I've noticed is the people with this virus move slowly. So, it's easier to maneuver around them. If you get too close they are able to move faster.

"Wren, we'll find Tex. He probably got free from the post and made his way home," Flynn tries to comfort me. "Tex always did want to eat. He never misses a meal."

"That damn horse is the only thing I've ever been able to keep in my life," the words come out but barely. "I've never thought of losing him until now and I just can't."

My chest hurts just saying those words. Tex has been the only consistent man in my life since I got him as a foal.

Flynn moves in front of me, just looking back for a moment. "Let's start at where you lay your head."

"Maybe you should follow me," I huff, pushing past him. "You don't know where to go."

Tex better have scurried home. Skullpass is a shitshow right now. If any one of these things has laid a hand or mouth on my horse, not even God will be able to stop me.

From behind me, I hear the sound of furniture scraping the floor. At least they are doing something I've asked. If only Flynn would have stayed inside, too. My stomach is aching, there's nothing in it but I want to throw up. I feel so hot, burning up from the inside out. My arm is throbbing from where I was bitten. Here I am, trying to be calm, looking for Tex.

"Fine then lead the way. We are wasting time." Flynn puts his hand out to me.

Guns still drawn, I try to avoid any of my townspeople who are walking slowly. I know that they aren't the people they once were but I just can't bring myself to finish them off. Flynn, on the other hand, has his guns going off behind me without fail. Bodies hitting the ground all around me.

"Wren, you need to get your head in the game. These are not the people you remember. They will kill you the first chance they get," Flynn whispers in my ear.

He's too close for comfort, bringing me back to when I invited him to be that close. Right now my skin is burning with every step I take. Even the blood in my veins itches. This virus is screaming to be released inside me.

Why haven't I turned yet?

Everyone else seems to have turned within a matter of minutes. I'm still holding out but not by much.

"Flynn," I breathe out as we draw close to my house. I can see it from here. Tears fill my sight as the pain is too much. "My place is on the end, you can't miss it. Take care of Tex," is all I can struggle to get out before the searing pain consumes me.

Chapter Nine

FLYNN

I've seen Wren in pain before. I've helped bandage wounds after knife fights and shootouts with her. She's a tough cookie, but this pain is like nothing I've seen cross her face before.

Her face contorts in pain as she slows down. Her words ring in my ears. 'Take care of Tex', she wouldn't give Tex up to anyone for any reason, if she is telling me to take care of him then she thinks she's going to die.

I step back as her knees hit the ground. Her hands on her hips as her breathing continues to be labored. The sweat on her face glimmering in the sunlight, more sweat than I've seen on her in a very long time. Not since the time she was sick all those years ago.

She had come down with a fever days before we were supposed to rob a train that was passing by. She thrashed in her sleep, fitful and sweating through clothes, as well as her bedding. Virgil and Holt were concerned, but if she couldn't do the job it wouldn't stop them from going on and not cutting her in.

The fever raged and subsided. She would be sweating and

soaking through clothes, then feel fine as soon as she threw up. It was like her body was fighting something more than a sickness. I stayed with her. Next to her. Trying to cool her skin with a wet cloth and being amazed by how hot her skin would be to the touch. No one I knew had ever had a fever so hot that it felt like it would burn you if you touched them.

The morning of the robbery, she emerged from her tent seeming completely better. She had breakfast with us and didn't mention anything more about the fever. It was as if it had never happened.

But it did and I remember the way her face looked as if the image was burned into my brain.

Wren is breathing harder now, to the point where I'm worried she might stop breathing. Squatting down next to her, I lean down trying to look at her face which has begun to hang down, her chin almost touching her chest.

My eyes trail down her arms as I notice the bandage again. Slowly, I reach forward and take her wrist in my hand. It's as if her skin is pure fire, like I've touched a hot iron, it's scorching. Still, I hold on and quickly find the end of the poorly-wrapped bandage. As I begin to unwind it, Wren takes a deep ragged breath and lifts her head slowly.

I look at her face and see it is no longer contorted in pain like it had been moments before. It seems clear, but the sweat still seems to pour off her skin, soaking her hairline and dripping off her face. Her eyes are closed, it's almost as if she is making peace with whatever is happening.

The bandage falls away from her arm and I look down at the wound that is red and raw beneath it. Teeth marks. The edges ripped and still bleeding a little.

She lied.

"God dammit, Wren," I mutter as I stare at the wound, rotating her wrist in my hand to see if there is anymore to it. "You reckless shit."

I let go of her wrist, watching it fall back down. Wren's face is still lifted as I stand back up looking down at her. My gun hangs loosely in my hand but I can't bring myself to raise it. I couldn't hurt her, I never could and I wouldn't start now.

I push my gun roughly back into my holster before bending down and grabbing her arm, throwing it over my shoulders and hauling her to her feet. She mumbles something I can't make out before I wrap my other arm around her waist.

"This shit is stupid even for you, Wren," I mutter, not sure she can even hear me. "I can't believe I found you after five years, only to lose you again because you decided to go all straight and narrow."

Wren mutters again as I begin to walk forward with her. Even through her clothes and mine, her skin is like fire. I can feel the heat through both of our clothes and I don't get more than twenty feet before I can feel her sweat soaking through my own clothes.

She doesn't help my efforts but she doesn't hinder them either. It's like she is conscious while being unconscious. Her muttering is becoming more constant, as well as more concerning. The hope is that I can make it to her place with her and before she turns.

I shake my head. I can't think like that. She will be fine. I keep saying that in my head, it's the one thought that will keep me going as I struggle to keep her in my grip. My focus stays on her house as we get closer, until I hear something in her muttering that is completely clear.

"Flynn," she says my name again.

But that voice only sounds slightly like her. Part of me wants to ignore it. That same part just wants to get her to the end of the road and see if Tex is there. Everything will be fine.

"Flynn." Her voice is stronger now.

I keep moving, but now she is starting to struggle against

my movement. Not fighting so much as trying to get my attention.

"Flynn," she says again, this time saying my name like she would when she was vexed with me.

It makes me stop in my tracks. I take a breath to steady myself for her to tell me to leave her. For her to tell me to end it before she turns. For me to tell her that I would rather die than take her life. I look at her face and noticed her eyes are open.

I suck in a breath and drop her arm from around my shoulders before taking a couple steps backward. Her eyes are open now and that fire I had seen earlier in them when she got angry, is burning bright in them again.

"Jesus, Wren, what is happening to you?" I sputter out.

"She's in pain right now, Flynn. The change takes a lot out of humans." The voice comes from Wren's mouth, but doesn't sound like Wren.

"What the fuck?" I say, narrowing my eyes. "What the hell is happening?"

"Wren was chosen from birth for this. She has managed to keep it hidden away and ignore me. But with all this," Wren motions around her and for a moment I remember what is happening. "She could no longer focus on keeping me locked away."

"You? What do you mean you? You are Wren," I say.

"Flynn, you are not as dumb as you make others think you are. She knows that, which means I know that. I look like her, because I am a part of her, but I am not Wren. I am what Wren needs to become in order to survive," she replies.

"Survive. So, you... um, she really did get infected when she was bitten?" I say.

"She was, but the change is already happening. It caused," she pauses, thinking for a moment, "the change to move faster. The virus cannot have Wren, when she already has a destiny."

"I don't understand what is happening. Where is Wren? What is going to happen to her?" I step closer. "Is she going to die?"

The smile that crosses Wren's face is one I have seen a hundred times. It's the smile she gives me when she thinks I am being dumb on purpose.

"Not today. But the change is going to happen soon and she needs to be clear from others. She is going to be weak and vulnerable afterward." The flames within her eyes brighten. "Take her home, but not into her home until after."

"After? After what?" I ask, feeling the panic renew in me.

Wren smiles at me. "You'll see. Now get moving."

As soon as she says it, Wren goes limp again. Lunging forward, I catch her before she hits the ground and I am starting to think she is going to burn out of her skin. Throwing her arm over my shoulder again, I start toward the house at the end of the street again. I could make it or at least as close to it as possible.

The heat radiating off her skin is starting to feel like it will burn me up as well. Sounds around us are getting louder and causing my skin to crawl. Wren moans beside me, the sweat coming off her in continuous lines. Gritting my teeth, I pull her tighter to me, focusing my eyes on the prize at the end.

A shade tree, outside of Tex's corral, where I can see him pacing back and forth in frantic movements.

"Damn, that horse is smart. He went back home. But who trapped him back in the corral?" I mutter to myself.

Tex whinnies the closer we get and Wren becomes heavier with each step toward the prized shade. It is ten trees away, then five, and Tex is losing his mind behind the rails. Three trees and I can hear movement behind me. I ignore it and focus on getting us to that final tree.

Wren drops to the ground under the shade tree as I hear the sound behind me. Turning and drawing my gun at the same time, I pull the trigger without registering who I am seeing. Until the body hits the ground. It's someone from town, someone I have seen walking around. With kids. I have no idea what her name is but I'm not sure it matters now anyway.

Behind me, Tex is kicking his corral rails and it causes me to turn toward him. Wren is writhing on the ground. Fingers digging into the dirt below her, mouth open as she gasps. I step toward her, stopping just as quickly. Flames lick across her arms. Those same flames that I saw in her eyes.

I start to look for a bucket to throw water on her when my name turns my eyes back to her.

"Flynn," The voice is weak but coming from Wren, "help her up. She needs to be on her feet."

Stepping closer, I reach down and grab Wren's arms, pulling her to her feet. The flames that danced over her skin biting into mine. As if giving a warning of what is about to happen. When she is on her feet, I take a moment to make sure she is steady before I tear my eyes from her to see what is coming up beside Tex.

Someone else has arrived and has eyes on Tex. Tex kicks the corral trying to scare off the thing. Blood drips from the person's neck as they try to reach Tex through the corral.

"Don't die. I have to go help Tex," I say to Wren, who doesn't even acknowledge I have said anything.

Stepping to the side of Wren, I lift my gun and fire a round into the person's head. They hit the corral and fall to the ground. Tex stands his ground as I move closer.

"Sorry 'bout that. Couldn't have anything happen to you while Wren is," I glance back before lifting the gun again, taking aim and shooting down another person, "whatever Wren is doing."

Tex doesn't seem to care what I have to say, he moves to the side of the corral that is more shaded and closer to the back. I don't know if he knows something I don't, but he seems to want to keep some space between what is about to happen and him.

Moving back to where I was in front of Wren, I notice that the flames that had seemed to be on the edges of her skin are consuming her entire body. Her face contorts in pain, but no sound is coming from her parted lips. Turning my back to her, I shoot another person stumbling out of the brush not far from us.

Behind me, the heat is becoming more intense, but I can't take my eyes off the road in case something comes at us. Tex alerts me twice that something is behind us during the fifteen minutes that follows.

It seems like an eternity.

And then it's like time stands still. I hear Wren let out a scream like I have never heard from her before. One that has my head whipping around to see if something is attacking her. The flames have consumed her entire body, burning away everything that would have made Wren exactly who she is.

She doesn't fight what is happening, but it doesn't seem like she is enjoying it, either. I stand transfixed, watching as the flames both consume her and leave her untouched at the same time. It's as if the fire is burning her from the inside out.

And that's when it hit me. Wren has no idea what is happening to her because it isn't something she knows could happen. Who would believe this if she told anyone? It is why I have to get her away from everyone. This would have been just shy of being called witchcraft to some.

The flames are burning brighter, burning hotter and all the while Wren stands there allowing them to cover her. When I shift, it's like it alerts her to my presence. Her eyes fly open and the fire behind them sends shivers down my spine. The raw power behind them causes me to take a step back from her.

Wren closes her eyes before letting her head tip back. The flames became too bright for me to keep looking at, causing me to raise my arms to shield my eyes.

And I can't have done it a moment too soon. When the last scream rips from her, it causes some sort of an explosion that pushes all that heat away from her and toward the world around her.

It knocks me flat on my back, my head hitting the ground with a hard smack. I hear Tex in the distance and part of me remembers that he is trapped in the corral. Ears ringing, I sit up to see Tex pushing against the rails, his head bobbing toward where Wren had been standing.

I am on my feet a second later, running toward the spot.

Chapter Ten

WREN

My eyes flitter open, my head is pounding. Everything is blurry, my whole body is heavy under my own weight. A moan comes from my lips and Flynn's face comes into focus as he's standing over me.

"What happened?" I manage to get out.

"You became a fireball," he tells me as he helps me sit up. "The flames around you kinda looked like a bird."

As my eyes finally adjust, I look around and find I'm in my house.

"Where's Tex?" I ask, finally sitting up.

"You and that damn horse," Flynn mumbles, giving me a head shake. "You don't care about yourself and being completely on fire?"

I try to stand, needing to see my horse. "Tex is the most important." I fall back onto the bed.

"You need to rest. I've got some food and water here for you to get your strength back." He hands it to me.

"Yeah, I'll pass on the water. That's how the virus is spread…" I cut my words off as I look at the bite on my arm.

There's nothing there. The bite is gone. My arm has none

of the scars on it that I've collected over the years. All the marks I've worn with pride. Each came with a story from a heist, many of them Flynn was involved in.

"This is safe," Flynn attempts to reassure me, trying to hand me a glass.

"Not going to happen." As I finally stand, my legs wobble a bit. "Take me to Tex then we need to check on everyone at the saloon."

"You were a fireball not even an hour ago," he protests, blocking my way. "You don't even have clothes on."

I don't cover myself since he's seen me naked for the last hour. "Why didn't you at least cover me up?"

"Well, the flames were still dancing on your skin a bit when I brought you inside, so I didn't want to set anything on fire," Flynn tells me as he rubs the back of his neck.

There's something he's not telling me, I can see it in his eyes. Then I remember I was in my favorite jeans. Those are gone now.

"Move so I can put on something. Everyone at the saloon is sitting ducks." I glare at him.

"But this view is oh so nice." Flynn is grinning.

With a shove, I push him out of my way. Little remnants of flames touch him. Flynn jumps back from my touch.

Flynn's voice trembles. "I knew you were hot, Wren, but didn't think you'd set me on fire."

"You said I was a fireball. Maybe I can control fire now." I shrug as I go to find something to wear.

My body doesn't feel like my own. My limp from being shot is gone, any aches I once had all have disappeared. I'm dressed before I know it. But where are my guns?

You don't need them, you have me.

"Who said that?" I stammer, looking around.

I am you. We are one. You've finally set me free so we can fly.

"I don't know what you mean." My voice comes out in a squeak.

You've hidden me away for so long, you don't even know what you are. Such a shame. We could have been doing so much more.

"Stop!" I scream holding my head.

I'll be here when you need me, Wren.

Flynn rushes into the room. "Wren, what's wrong?"

"Everything," I mumble, pushing past him as I go to check on Tex.

Tex whinnies as he sees me approaching, stepping back a little before finally realizing it's me. My heart skips a beat when he doesn't know it's me, but he gives me a nudge that's him telling me he does after a moment.

"Stay here," I tell Tex, giving him a pat on top of his nose. "I've got to go make sure everybody in town's fine."

He nods his head yes, like he knows what I'm saying.

"Wren," Flynn's voice comes from behind me. "Those things are getting close to the house again. If we are going, we need to move now."

"Fine," I huff, looking away from Tex. I'm hopeful this won't be the last time I'll see him.

Over half the town is turned and roaming openly at what seems to be dawn now. Flynn never told me how long I was out for. With no weapons, I beeline it right to Golden Gait to make sure everyone is okay.

The front doors are swinging back and forth, dripping in blood. My voice is stuck in my throat, if I do yell, all those things will come this way. So, I stop myself, not drawing any more attention to us.

"Wren," Flynn says from behind me.

I spin around so fast my head almost spins twice. "Sshhh. They have made it inside. We don't want to bring anymore here to us."

CHAPTER TEN · 65

The inside of the Golden Gait is a mess. Bodies and blood everywhere. Right off, I don't see Levi or Adeline. Holt on the other hand didn't make it. Looks like he didn't make it out of his chair before they were overrun. Bite marks all up and down his arms. His neck is all gone. Chunks taken from his face. I can barely tell it is him, if it hadn't been for his clothes, I'm not sure I would have.

Holt's guns are still holstered, I can use them since he can't. As I reach for them, fire shoots from my fingers.

"Fine, no guns," I say to myself.

You have me now. We are the weapon.

I'm so confused. "What does that mean, 'weapon?'"

"Who are you talking to?" Flynn asks, looking perplexed as he grabs Holt's guns.

"Myself... like I always have," I mumble. "Why are you following up my butt? We need to make sure the rest of them are safe."

I trek up to the second floor as Flynn checks the back rooms on the first floor. The Golden Gait has five rooms, I kick in the first door I come to; no one, so I continue down the line. Each door is more of the same. Holding my breath as I get to the last one, once it's kicked in—nothing. No bodies, no people. Where did they go?

"Nothing down here," Flynn calls up to me.

If I was down there he'd get hit in the face for that. Every noise we make is a call for those things out there. A flame wafts from one of my fingers and I see it go over the banister down toward Flynn. I hear him let out a yelp a couple moments later. A little smile tugs at my mouth but not for long, not knowing where my friends are.

It's time to go back down to Flynn and then figure out where they went to hide. We do have a church here but I've never seen any of them step foot in it.

As I hit the last couple of steps, I let Flynn know our next moves. "Let's check the sheriff's office, maybe being behind bars could be the safest place for anyone."

"Or the stupidest." He laughs under his breath.

The front doors slam open, bringing my eyes to them, three people stagger in. They aren't themselves and likely to bite us. Flynn wastes no time firing his guns. He hits two of the three dead center of the head. The third, he hits in the neck. A bit of blood spews from the hole but that doesn't stop him. Before I know it, one of my hands is pointing at the once man and a flame launches out, hitting him in the chest then spreading rapidly all over his body.

Chapter Eleven

Flynn and I stand watching as the shell of a man slumps to the ground. The flames dance over his skin even as his charred body twitches one last time. Flynn looks at me, guns still ready. Shrugging, I step over the charred corpse of one of the people I swore to protect before starting toward the front door.

Flynn raises his guns, shooting as we make our way down the main street. If any of the things get too close, my hands raise and fire engulfs them. I don't decide when to release the fire, it just happens.

Between the two of us, we make it to the sheriff's office pretty quickly, leaving a trail of dead, or rather deader, bodies behind us. As I reach for the door knob of the office, I try to turn it and am met with resistance. Something is blocking the door.

I raise a fist and pound on the door.

"Adeline! I hope to hell you are in there!" I yell, banging once more on the door to punctuate my demand.

From behind the door I hear scraping and Flynn raises his gun again. He has spent a few seconds emptying the spent casings and reloading again. The door cracks open enough to show Adeline's face and I am sure my heart will burst from relief.

"Wren." She looks me over before glancing at Flynn. "You okay?"

"Better now that I see you are safe. I thought I told you to stay put?" I reply.

"Those things came inside or maybe they were inside. We had to get out." She shrugs. "Figured if nothing else, we could lock ourselves in the cell and be safe there."

"Not sure being in the jail cell is safe, but at least you're alright." I peek over her head, trying to see inside. "Who else we got?"

"Not many." Adeline steps back from the door and I can hear muffled voices before more scraping, then the door opens wider. "Get inside before those things find us."

Adeline motions me inside and I grab a hold of Flynn, dragging him inside as well. Once the door is closed and my heavy desk pressed against the door again, I look around to see who is still there. Relief washes over me as I spot Levi in the corner with a couple kids. He's safe. Buck and Edgar have weapons at the ready standing watch at the windows. Daisy is sitting in one of the cells on the bed trying to comfort someone but I can't see who. Half a dozen or more people are standing or sitting in various places in the room.

Looking back to Adeline, I can feel the frown. "This everyone?"

"Everyone we could find on the way here that wasn't sick," she replies quietly.

Geez, this is everyone who is left in town. Town of almost 200 people, down to a little over a dozen. What the fuck is happening? Flynn has taken up a post at one of the windows and I can feel the heat still running below my skin but it's like the flames know it would scare those around me.

But I have to tell Adeline. Someone besides Flynn needs to know what is going on with me. In case things get crazy before I can explain myself.

"Adie, I need to tell you something," I say, turning my back to the room.

"You aren't sick are you?" Adie asks, raising concerned eyes to my face.

I smile a little. "No, I'm not sick. I don't think I can get sick anymore."

"Then whatever it is, we will get through it together. Like a family," Adeline says, laying a hand on my arm before lifting it immediately. "Christ, Wren, your skin is like fire."

"Yeah, that's what I need to talk to you about." I glance over my shoulder before taking a deep breath. "Just try not to freak out until I'm done, okay?"

Adeline quirks an eyebrow at me but gives me a nod. With a steadying breath, I tell her what happened and then tell her what Flynn told me. Adeline doesn't move, she doesn't so much as blink as I'm telling her about what happened, even the part about hearing the voice in my head. When I'm done, I stand, waiting for her to tell me I'm crazy or that I've lost my mind. Instead, she says the thing I would never have expected.

Grinning at me, she shakes her head. "Always knew there was something special about you, Wren."

"That's all you have to say?" I stare at her, shocked.

"Wren, before you came to town we had a quiet life here. Nothing really ever happened. Every so often, we would have some issues with the boys who wander in from the mines." She shrugs. "But for the most part, life was boring." Adie looks at me with a smile. "When you showed up, it was like the entire town shifted. You brought something with you that brought life back to the town. Sure, there was more danger as more miners showed up, but we all knew you would handle them. There wasn't a day that went by that we didn't feel safe."

I turn to lean against the desk. "Doesn't bother you that I could burst into flames?"

"You'd never hurt your own people, Wren. Not if you could help it," Adie says.

She's right, that voice in my head chimes in.

"Then we save our town. Or what's left of it." Looking around the room, I know I can't let anything happen to the people in it.

I can help with that.

"Oh, you're going to," I mumble.

"What was that?" Adie asks.

"Just, talking to the voice in my head." The smile I give Adie shows how crazy that sounded.

"Well, okay. Make sure you keep our people safe. That's your job, Sheriff." Adeline gives me a wink before pushing off the desk, making her way toward Buck and Edgar.

Flynn steps up next to me as I process what Adeline said. It's my job to protect them, but how can I protect them when what is harming them is what we need to survive? Water is a very important thing that we need to survive and water seems to be out to kill us all.

I let my head hang for a moment. The feeling of defeat creeping in. Flynn nudges my shoulder with his arm.

"So, how are we going to get out of this sticky situation?" he asks.

"Why is it always my job to save your ass?" I smile, before looking up at him.

"Because that's what friends do. It's what family does for each other." He looked around the room, causing me to do so as well. "This might be just a bunch of townspeople, but they are your family now, Wren. They need your protection." Flynn looks at me again.

"Well, first things first, we need to get rid of all the infected people. Letting them roam out there is only going to cause more problems. After we get rid of all those who have been turned into those monsters, we can search for survivors. Then we can figure out how the hell we all survive when the water is what's turning us all into those monsters." I push off the desk onto my feet again. "Guess we need a plan to get all those infected into one place."

Flynn grins at me. "I have an idea."

"And I have a feeling I'm going to hate it." I shake my head as he starts talking.

"For the record, I would like to make it known that this is a bad idea," Adeline says for the tenth time.

"We know, Adie. But we don't have many options. We need to get rid of the infected and find out who else may have survived," I remind her.

"Still don't have to like it." Adie says, shaking her head.

"Unless you got a better idea," I pause, watching her let out a sigh. "Then this is the best option for now."

"I'll make a run for the church first. You go for Tex. I'll draw as many as I can," Flynn says, like I need a reminder.

"You stay safe. Stay alive." I point a finger at him. "I mean it."

His grin spreads. "Yes, ma'am."

Buck and Edgar are standing at the door, ready to move the desk again to let us out. They are staying behind to guard the others, which they aren't happy with either.

The desk grinds against the floor as they drag it back

enough for Flynn and I to slip out the door again. Adeline gives me one last look before closing the door behind us. I know the look. It means come back safe or my ass is history.

Flynn takes my hand and gives it a squeeze before starting down the steps onto the main street. Turning the opposite way I sprint toward my home and Tex who's waiting for me. Behind me, I can hear sounds and groans, before Flynn's voice is heard calling as loud as he can.

It drives the sounds coming from behind me in that direction. I can see Tex ahead, pacing in his corral. Reaching the gate, I open it as Tex comes toward me. He nudges my shoulder as he passes through the gate. I check the straps on both sides of his saddle before mounting him.

"You aren't going to like what we gotta do," I mutter, running a hand over his neck.

Tex shakes beneath me and stomps his hooves. He's ready to take on whatever is out there with me, just as we always have.

"Alright, if you are still in there, I'm sure you know the plan. Tex stays safe, though. Flynn, too." I know if anyone saw me they would think I was crazy, talking to myself.

I'm always here. I know what we need to do. Just get us there.

Still creeps me out, but if it will save the town and the people left, I can accept it. I tap Tex's side to get him moving and he takes off in a trot.

In the distance, I can hear Flynn and I move Tex in the opposite direction. We need to round them up from all around town and get them to the church.

Rounding a corner, I see a group wandering slowly around. A sharp whistle grabs their attention and suddenly, Tex is backing up. Turning him, we head back toward the main street, the small group growing larger with each sharp whistle I let loose.

At the other end of the road, I can see Flynn, running as

fast as he can toward the edge of town. The group behind him is gaining quick, but he will make it. A glance behind me does nothing but shatter my heart. All the people in town that have become something inhuman, all those people I was supposed to protect.

Facing forward again, I tap Tex again, spurring him on a little faster. We reach the church before Flynn or either group and I swing down at the steps. The doors to the church are wide open and I hear something that makes my stomach roll.

From inside the doors, the preacher stumbles out. Blood dripping from his lips, his kind eyes no longer seeing anything beyond whatever is driving these things on.

"Well, that's unfortunate," I mumble as Flynn comes to a sudden stop beside me.

"You want me to handle that?" Flynn asks, reaching for his gun.

"No, she will," I reply, letting my hand raise toward him.

The flames appear as if summoned and the preacher is consumed by them within seconds. Crumpling onto the steps of the church, his body contorts as it burns.

Flynn looks at me. "You are kind of terrifying, you know that, right?"

"I've always been terrifying. You've just always been on my side." I smirk at him. "Now, you know your part. Get Tex outta here."

"I still—" Flynn starts.

"We don't have time." I motion to the mass of people, or what were once townspeople, making their way toward us. "It's a shitty plan, but it's the only one we have. She will keep me safe and you will keep Tex safe." Grabbing the front of his shirt I pull him closer to me, flames dancing at my fingertips. "You keep both of you safe."

Flynn reaches a hand up to cover mine. The flames touch

his skin but he doesn't flinch away. Leaning forward, he presses his lips to mine only for a second before pulling away.

"She keeps you safe and you come back to us," he says before dropping his hand away.

Tex tries to back away as Flynn grabs the saddle. He understands that Flynn is taking him away from me and he is not happy about it. The flames rise off my skin as the horde comes closer. Flynn turns Tex, riding away from town so none of the infected turn back to follow him.

We didn't need to worry, though. I was bait enough for them. Standing in the open, flames dancing across my skin, it was like giving them an easy meal. The heat inside me returns, but this time I'm not afraid. It doesn't scare me. I'm going to embrace whatever I have become, if it means I can save anyone in town.

Walking backwards till my boots hit the steps of the church, I draw them toward me. Some missing limbs, most dripping blood from somewhere on them, all of them with those eyes that see nothing like they did before. Taking another step back, I slowly climb the steps till I'm at the top.

Below me the horde is coming closer and is exactly where I want them to be. The flames that have begun to cover my entire body don't seem to distract them at all from their goal. With one last look around at the people who I failed to protect I surrender control to the fire within me.

"I'm so sorry I couldn't protect you all," I whisper, tears rolling down my cheeks before the overwhelming heat takes over.

This time when the flames come from me, I can see it all. The flames spread from one person to another, jumping and sliding across skin and hair. It's like watching gunpowder ignite, the line might break but it never stops as the flame moves from one spot to the next.

It isn't long until the entire horde is on fire and still

coming toward me. I keep moving backward, drawing them into the open church behind me. Even burning, their skin charring and crackling, they follow me in.

They begin dropping to the floor as the pews catch fire. The wood pops with the burning heat. The rug that runs from the doors to the pulpit catching fire as they drag themselves over each other trying to reach me.

I stand at the front of the church, in the same spot the preacher would give his Sunday sermons, talking about the devil and how he would consume us all with fire for our sins. Standing there, I watch as those same townspeople fall down covered in flames. Some make sounds like they might still have some of their right minds, but most continue trying to get to me.

It doesn't take long for the building to be completely covered in flames. It takes about the same amount of time for the roof to begin to crumble above us. I watch as it begins to collapse and crushes a few people, allowing the flames something else to catch onto.

The church is burning to the ground around them and they don't even care. That is how I know that these are no longer the people I am supposed to protect. These are the things that I have to protect my people from. A thought I never realized is so true to me.

I would protect them, with my life.

Epilogue

1 YEAR LATER

As I sit rocking on the porch of the sheriff's station looking at the hustle and bustle of the town I almost lost not that long ago, I'm happy to see how far we've come together to rebuild it. We've already got a new church up and running. The townfolk that survived put more faith in Him helping than anything else. They think the fire within me is a miracle from the almighty above. For myself, I'm not sure. I've always felt her presence but was too afraid to let her out, but now as the power is free, I feel whole.

The water seemed fine after my firey display in the church. Maybe it burned hot enough close to the well to kill off whatever was in the water. I'm not sure.

Flynn stayed in Skullpass with me, finally deciding to give up the old life and is my deputy. Him sharing my bed with me is a nice bonus.

The Golden Gait is back to business as usual. Adeline's doing what she does best and even has some new girls working there. Daisy gave up that life, married Levi of all of the men. They are expecting a child anytime now.

"Logan!" I yell as he's running to me with a paper in hand, his face drained of blood. "What's wrong?"

"I got one word from this telegram. Not sure what to make of it. It can't be right. But it just kept repeating," Logan rambles on.

"Well what is it, boy?" I demand, a bit annoyed he's not getting to the point."

He hands me the paper. One word is on it over and over.

Werewolves

The End

About Jupiter Dresden

Jupiter is just a small town girl with big dreams. She loves to travel with her husband. She's a mother & cat lover. Anything paranormal has always fascinated her, as well as writing, so it's only natural she'd mix the two.

You can follow her here:

Facebook:
Jupiters Journey
Amazon:
Jupiter Dresden
Instagram:
authorjupiterdresden
TikTok:
@authorjupiterdresden

Acknowledgments

First I'd like to thank my mom for always being behind me no matter what.

A big thank you to my husband for being with me on this crazy ride and supporting me every step of the way.

And I want to send a special shout out to vent buddy and all around sister now. Victoria thank you for everything you do and always being there for me.

I huge shout out to my beta readers for all you do! Thank You Melody, Alicia, Christine & Katy. You guys keep me going.

Thank you to my support system that a can pop in and ask if something sounds good. Crystal, Jenée, Emily, Tammi, Kasey, B, Roxanne, Cassie & Steph.

And a big thank you to all the people that let me use them as my character inspiration! (And maybe kill them.)

And Thank you Averi for the Beautiful cover and Michelle for all your hard work editing my book so fast.

Also by Jupiter Dresden

The Curse Of Winchester

Operation Ann

Gifted Curse (Co-write with Rinna Ford)

Goddess Of Flames

Hunter (Co-write with Jenée Robinson)

Abandon Hope (Co-write with Jenée Robinson & Evelyn Belle)

Sam's Secret

Hidden Truths Of Ravenwood

Defending Skullpass (Co-write with Evelyn Belle)

Sinners Playground (April 2024)

Anthologies:

Melissa & The Lost Tomb of Akila

Always Dreaming

With This Axe

Mania's Death (Co-write with Miki Ward)

A Date With Death (Co-write with M. Lizbeth)

Drina

My Zombie Girlfriend

Heart Of A Hunter

About Evelyn Belle

Evelyn is a stay at home mom to four kids in the mountains of Southern California. When she isn't writing she is attempting to catching up on her TBR pile. Her obsessions run deep and when she decides she likes something she is all in. A fan girl, just like everyone else.

Her first novella titled 'Song of the Seas' is available on Amazon, with a sequel in the works. Defending Skullpass isn't her first short story. She has written a few now and has co-written with Jenee Robinson and Jupiter Dresden before. Her most recent work was a short in Abandon Hope, an all female pirate crew.

To keep in touch with her and follow her upcoming works, find her here:

www.facebook.com/groups/evelynscalltothedeep/

Also By Evelyn Belle

Song of the Seas (Siren Tales Book 1)
Slayer of Monsters: The Quest for Medusa's Head
Abandon Hope: Tale's From The Hope's Shipmen

Made in the USA
Monee, IL
20 October 2023

44885730R00058